The Underlying Chris

by Will Eno

FOR PRODUCTION ENQUIRIES

UNITED STATES AND CANADA
info@concordtheatricals.com
1-866-979-0447

UNITED KINGDOM AND EUROPE
licensing@concordtheatricals.co.uk
020-7054-7200

Each title is subject to availability from Concord Theatricals Corp., depending upon country of performance. Please be aware that *THE UNDERLYING CHRIS* may not be licensed by Concord Theatricals Corp. in your territory. Professional and amateur producers should contact the nearest Concord Theatricals Corp. office or licensing partner to verify availability.

---

be invented, including mechanical, electronic, photocopying, recording, videotaping, or otherwise, without the prior written permission of the publisher. No one shall upload this title(s), or part of this title(s), to any social media websites.

For all enquiries regarding motion picture, television, and other media rights, please contact Concord Theatricals Corp.

MUSIC USE NOTE

Licensees are solely responsible for obtaining formal written permission from copyright owners to use copyrighted music in the performance of this play and are strongly cautioned to do so. If no such permission is obtained by the licensee, then the licensee must use only original music that the licensee owns and controls. Licensees are solely responsible and liable for all music clearances and shall indemnify the copyright owners of the play(s) and their licensing agent, Concord Theatricals Corp., against any costs, expenses, losses and liabilities arising from the use of music by licensees. Please contact the appropriate music licensing authority in your territory for the rights to any incidental music.

IMPORTANT BILLING AND CREDIT REQUIREMENTS

If you have obtained performance rights to this title, please refer to your licensing agreement for important billing and credit requirements.

THE UNDERLYING CHRIS premiered in New York City, produced by Second Stage Theater (Carole Rothman, President and Artistic Director; Casey Reitz, Executive Director), on November 21, 2019. The production was directed by Kenny Leon, with scenic design by Arnulfo Maldonado, costume design by Dede Ayite, lighting design by Amith Chandrashaker, and sound design by Dan Moses Schreier. The stage manager was Samantha Watson. The cast was as follows:

CHRISTINE & OTHERS	Isabella Russo
MOTHER & OTHERS	Hannah Cabell
LISA & OTHERS	Nidra Sous La Terre
TOPHER & OTHERS	Howard Overshown
GABRIELLA & OTHERS	Lenne Klingaman
PHILIP & OTHERS	Nicholas Hutchinson
KRISTA & OTHERS	Lizbeth Mackay
KIT & OTHERS	Michael Countryman
PAUL & OTHERS	Luis Vega
BARBARA & OTHERS	Denise Burse
REGGIE & OTHERS	Charles Turner

THE UNDERLYING CHRIS was originally co-commissioned by Center Theatre Group (Michael Ritchie, Artistic Director; Stephen Rountree, Managing Director) and Second Stage Theater (Carole Rothman, Artistic Director; Casey Reitz, Executive Director).

CHARACTERS

In the world-premiere production, directed by Kenny Leon, the defining characteristic of the cast was a very human, natural, and unfussy approach to acting. An incredible specificity, that was expressed with a very light touch. The cast was diverse and the diversity told the story in a way that Kenny and I found compelling and meaningful. I am including race in the character descriptions below to ensure diversity of the cast and as a helpful (I hope) guide to assembling a strong and inclusive ensemble.

Here is a simplified list of actors, in an eleven-person cast, in order of appearance:

CHRISTINE & OTHERS – female, 10-12, Asian-American
MOTHER & OTHERS – female, thirties/forties, white
LISA & OTHERS – thirties/forties, Black
TOPHER & OTHERS – male, thirties/forties, Black
GABRIELLA & OTHERS – female, twenties, white
PHILIP & OTHERS – male, 10-12, Black or Hispanic
KRISTA & OTHERS – female, sixties, white
KIT & OTHERS – male, sixties, white
PAUL & OTHERS – male, thirties, Hispanic
BARBARA & OTHERS – female, sixties/seventies, Black
REGGIE & OTHERS – male, seventies, Black

AUTHOR'S NOTES

With respect to casting, all kinds of people should be included, so that the play resembles the world. Maximum diversity and difference are crucial to the structure of the play, especially in casting the "Chris" characters, who we will meet in roughly chronological order, though they will be changing constantly in terms of gender, race, etc. This is as much for the purposes of theatricality, energy, and surprise as for a social or political message; though, that said, it's hoped that the play expresses a basic spirit of inclusiveness and commonality. A further hope is that simply following the story will be an act of and an exercise in empathy for the audience. Maybe that is true of all plays.

Doubling of roles:

There is ample opportunity to double-cast many of these roles. A scene-by-scene breakdown follows, with suggested doubling.

With an eleven-person cast, the doubling might work something like this:

PROLOGUE – female, 10-12 [**CHRISTINE**]

Scene One

MOTHER – thirties
NURSE – thirties/forties [**KRISTIN**]
FATHER – thirties

Scene Two

NANNY – female, twenties
CHRIS – male, 10

Scene Three

CHRISTINE – female, 12-14
JUSTINE – forties [**MOTHER**]
DR. RIVINGTON – male, forties [**FATHER**]

Scene Four

RADIO HOST – male, sixties [**KIT**]
ADVERTISEMENT ACTOR – female, forties [**KRISTIN**]
RADIO PRODUCER – female, sixties [**KRISTA**]
KRIS – 21 [**NANNY**]

Scene Five

CHRISTOPHER – male, late twenties/early thirties
LOUISE – female, late twenties/early thirties [**MOTHER**]
CAFÉ EMPLOYEE [**NANNY**]

Scene Six

LOUIS – forties [**FATHER**]
KRISTIN – female, forties [voice of **NURSE**]
JOAN – 16 [**CHRISTINE**]
PAUL [**CHRISTOPHER**]
HELPER [**NANNY**]

Scene Seven

DIRECTOR'S VOICE – female, sixties/seventies [**CHRISTIANA**]
TOPHER – fifties [**FATHER**]
RODERICK – fifties [**KIT**]
SOUND DESIGNER'S VOICE [**CHRISTOPHER**]
LIGHTING DESIGNER'S VOICE [**MOTHER**]
CREW PERSON [**NANNY**]
WARDROBE PERSON [**CHRISTINE**]

Scene Eight

KRISTA – sixties [**RADIO PRODUCER**]
PHILIP – male, 10-12 [**CHRIS**]
CHRISTOPH – male, seventies
JOAN 2 [**KRISTIN**]

Scene Nine

DMV PATRON 1 [**CHRISTINE**]
DMV PATRON 2 [**CHRISTOPHER**]
DMV PATRON 3 [**FATHER**]
JOAN 2 [**KRISTIN**]
KIT – male, seventies
DMV EMPLOYEE [**KRISTA**]

Scene Ten

LISA [**KRISTIN**]
CHRISTIANA – female, 82
MOTHER [**MOTHER**]
GABRIELLA [**NANNY**]

Scene Eleven

KHRIS – male, eighties
LANGLEY [**NANNY** or **KRISTIN**]

Scene Twelve

JUNE [**MOTHER**]
JAKE [**FATHER**]
POLLY [**NANNY**]
MIKEY [**CHRIS**]
BEN [**CHRISTOPHER**]
MARTHA [**KRISTIN**]
EVA [**KRISTA**]
BARBARA [**CHRISTIANA**]
GORDON [**KIT**]
REGGIE [**KHRIS**]
ALLISON [**CHRISTINE**]

A note on set design:
Transitions should happen quickly and organically, with the play flowing, as much as possible, from scene to scene. Specificity, but with economy and some sly elegance. There should be a feeling of things tumbling forward, rather than a stop-and-start feeling of sets being changed. The play should also feel as if it's opening up as it moves forward, though it then might seem to close down, in Scenes Nine through Eleven, before Scene Twelve, which should have the most wide-open and natural feel of any of the scenes.

A note on sound design:
Subtle sound can and should be used for transitions. One possibility with respect to sound, used to great effect in the premiere production, is to use sounds that might thematically fit with the upcoming scene as the transition sound *into* that scene. An example: a splashing sound could be used going from Scene One to Scene Two, in which we will hear about pools and diving. Another example: a sound of galloping horses could take us from Scene Four to Scene Five, in which we will hear about animals and veterinary medicine. This is a very specific idea, but the larger global idea is to use all aspects of production in a subtle and thoughtful way that supports and enhances the feelings and ideas of the play and contributes to its forward motion.

A note on costume design:
When roles are double-cast and triple-cast, costume changes should be quick and efficient, while being as convincing as possible. Actors should not make broad or showy efforts to differentiate between multiple characters they might be playing, nor should the production. In fact, all the "Chris" actors should share a single simple gesture or trait – nothing too obvious, in fact it's fine if some audience members miss it.

A general note:
It is both a reasonable and metaphysical question as to how much time passes in the play. Keeping the costume and design choices simple and relatively "timeless" might allow for a greater and richer interpretation of this matter.

To the one and only Albertine

PROLOGUE

Spotlight up on a girl, age eleven or so, in a well-fitting (but not perfect-fitting) men's suit with tie. She is confident and relaxed, and entirely comfortable in her gestures, hesitations, and choice of words. In one hand, she holds a pen and a used envelope with some notes written on it, which she will glance at from time to time.

PROLOGUE. Hi, hello – a few quick thoughts before we get going. *(To a person in the audience who may be turning his or her phone off:)* Oh, perfect, just reminded me, thank you – phones off, beeping watches, sounds of the outside world, all that. Exits – they're right there, underneath the signs that say "Exit." *(Looks up.)* That's the ceiling. There's no sign on it but maybe you were able to recognize it on your own. That's basically everything. Oh, no photos. You'll just have to try to remember what happened.

A quick peak at her envelope notes.

As for the play, the subject is life on Earth. I hope everything is familiar-enough to be followable, but, foreign-enough to be fun. That was a lot of F sounds, there.

A little more specifically, our story is – it's a story about, let's see...

She is not lost but merely trying to find the best words to use.

Identity? Change, maybe. Continuality, if that's a word. Newness and renewal. Those are words. It's a story about the moments that shape a life, and the people

1

who shape a moment. And the things we *don't* have names for. The essence, I guess, the spirit. And also, mystery. And, meaning.

The three following parts should be kept together so they subtly build, and not divided up into two separate questions and a request:

Who's up for some meaning?! Do things have meaning?! Sisters and brothers, let me hear you say "Yeahhhh!"

On "Yeahhhh," she does a very small, very restrained version of the "roof raising" gesture or raising a hand. She puts a hand on her lower back.

Augghh, just felt a little twinge. You ever do that? A tiny little movement in the just-wrong direction? Did I just describe a career choice or marriage you're familiar with? We're all so fragile.

She takes a small breath, to relax her back.

I'm not as young as I used to be. It's true.

She stands – maybe with both hands on her lower back to give it support – in a relaxed and confident pose.

Anyway, the play begins in a crib. Like with evolution, and most other good ideas, we will go forward looking backward, not knowing our destination until the day we get there, or years later or never.

This is the journey of a certain Chris through the world, through time and places and doors. The formative minutes, the pauses, the speechless years, the little touches. *(Very brief pause.)* Maybe this play is going to be a little place on your map, someday. Imagine – years from right now, you look back. "And then one time I saw a play that had a name in the title – Stacy maybe or Lee – and, I'll never forget, I felt such-and-such. I was there, I was definitely me but younger, and I felt such-and-such." We would be honored to be even partly remembered like that. *(Tiny little moment where she holds her back or adjusts her stance. Offhandedly, to a person in the third row:)* Make sure you stretch. Thank you.

　　Lights change.

Scene One
Modest room in a modest house. Evening.

> **MOTHER** *(thirties) is on the phone with a* **NURSE** *(female, offstage).*

MOTHER. Three months old, in a week.

> *She looks into the bassinet. Quietly, with love:*

Hi, Chris.

NURSE. *(Offstage:)* And he ate bad carrots?

MOTHER. No, he was playing with a stuffed toy carrot and it touched his eye, and he sort of twisted and I think he hurt his back.

NURSE. *(Offstage, writing this down:)* "Playing with big toy carrot."

> **MOTHER** *switches to using the hands-free speaker option and sets the phone down, adjusts the baby's blanket, etc.*

MOTHER. When I lift him up, I feel a little click.

NURSE. *(Offstage:)* Babies click sometimes. Is he in distress?

MOTHER. Oh, I hope not. He's smiling. I just want him to fall asleep.

NURSE. *(Offstage:)* Okay. Please hold.

MOTHER. *(To herself, quietly:)* "Distress."

> *Some Muzak quietly plays.* **MOTHER** *eats some food from a takeout container. A small, vowel-ly sound comes from the bassinet:*

---

*A license to produce *The Underlying Chris* does not include a performance license for any third-party or copyrighted music. Licensees should create an original composition or use music in the public domain. For further information, please see Music Use Note on page 3.

BABY IN BASSINET. Heeaah.

MOTHER. *(Lovingly and calmly:)* How very interesting, Christopher. Tell me more. I hope you'll tell me more, over the next fifty years.

>   *She holds up her fork.*

"Fork." You'll use one of these, one day.

>   *She takes a bite and looks at her fork.*

It's actually a pretty good invention.

>   *She stares into the bassinet.*

NURSE. *(Offstage:)* We can see you tomorrow. Hello? *(Brief pause.)* Are you still there?

MOTHER. Yes, sorry. I'm not getting much sleep.

NURSE. *(Offstage, with a simple and dry sense of humor:)* Is that the one where you close your eyes while your husband kicks you? My kids are two and six.

MOTHER. I can't imagine.

NURSE. *(Offstage:)* Yes, you can.

MOTHER. Maybe.

NURSE. *(Offstage:)* The other day I forgot the word for "elbow."

MOTHER. Yeah, make sure you write that one down.

NURSE. *(Offstage:)* We can see you tomorrow at 11:15.

MOTHER. Oh, that's great. *(Writing:)* 11:15.

>   *She smiles into the bassinet and speaks quietly to the baby:*

Close your eyes, Chris. *(To **NURSE**:)* I just want her to be okay.

NURSE. *(Offstage:)* Yeah, of course.

>   **FATHER** *(thirties) enters, puts down his keys, bag, etc.* **MOTHER** *waves hello.* **FATHER** *smiles and goes off into another room.*

MOTHER. He keeps fussing but I know he wants to sleep. To rest. Oh, look at you in there. *(Gazing at baby:)* He's so little. His little back.

NURSE. *(Offstage:)* The littleness is the thing I can't get over. The little fingernails. A tiny little thigh bone in there somewhere. *(Very brief pause.)* We'll see you tomorrow. *(A mangled echo, a technological phone glitch:)* It's always good to be certain, good tain tain cer cer cer, good.

MOTHER. Did you hear that?

NURSE. *(Offstage:)* What?

MOTHER. An echo or something.

NURSE. *(Offstage:)* Well, we're talking over wires and beams of light. A glitch in the miracle is still part of the miracle. See you tomorrow. *(Answering a call, as she's ending this one:)* Hello, Northfield Medical Group, how may –

    (**MOTHER** *ends the call.*)

FATHER. *(Offstage:)* Everything all right?

MOTHER. Come say hi.

FATHER. *(Offstage:)* Washing my hands.

MOTHER. *(Gently, to baby:)* That's your daddy. Washing his hands.

    She holds up her hand.

"Hand." "Fork." Another hundred words and you could sell real estate. *(To* **FATHER**, *as he enters:)* He really missed you. He pointed at the door. He even made a sound that sounded like "door."

FATHER. Awww. I don't think he can see that far.

MOTHER. His eyes are perfect.

FATHER. I'm not saying he's blind. Just, we go through stages. Fuzzy, clear, too clear, fuzzy. *(To baby:)* Do you think Daddy is a door? Señor Christopher! Hello, Mr. Chris.

    FATHER *and* **MOTHER** *kiss.*

MOTHER. Sort of a rough afternoon.

FATHER. Oh no.

MOTHER. He twisted funny and now his back is making a little click.

FATHER. *(Lovingly:)* Oh, my darling Kit. Did you throw your tiny back out?

MOTHER. I hope it's not the way you fly him around the room.

FATHER. Babies love flying around like that. I just want him to feel himself moving. Motion. *(To baby:)* Hi, Chris. You can do it, whatever it is, whenever it comes.

MOTHER. I got an appointment for tomorrow.

FATHER. Didn't his ankle make a little sound, right when he was born?

MOTHER. Yeah, but this is from something. That just started out of nowhere.

FATHER. Things don't just start out of nowhere.

> **MOTHER** *looks into the crib.*

MOTHER. Where do they start?

FATHER. I have a really weird headache.

> *He exits into the other room.*

MOTHER. Drink some water.

FATHER. *(From offstage, an indecipherable version of "I'm exhausted":)* Ahma zost.

MOTHER. What? *(Brief pause.)* Do you want some aspirin or something?

> *She gazes into the bassinet. Quietly:*

You've had a big day. You just rest up, Chrissie. The days are a lot bigger than you right now, but you'll grow. *(Quietly, to* **FATHER** *in the other room:)* Can you go with us tomorrow? *(Brief pause.)* Honey? *(Brief pause.)* Richard? Sweetie?

> *Lights.*

Scene Two
Modest living room. Late afternoon.

> **NANNY** *(a Polish woman, twenties) is picking up some toys. One is a faded stuffed toy carrot.*

NANNY. Chris, please help me clean. We have to bring these little things up.

> **CHRIS** *(ten-year-old boy) enters, holding a flower by the stem, like it's an airplane.*

CHRIS. Vrooommmm. Dddzzzooommm. *(Quietly, to himself:)* Oh no, Captain, engine trouble, engine trouble.

> *He crash-lands the flower.*

NANNY. This is a flower plane?

CHRIS. No, it's a plane that's a flower. *(Machine-gun noises:)* Tft-tft-tft-tft-tft.

NANNY. Help, please. I am only beginning this job. I want to do a good impression.

> **CHRIS** *picks up some toys.* **NANNY** *gets a call on her cell phone. She speaks in Polish:*

Pracuje jeszcze przez dwie godziny. Tak, chlopak bez ojca. Spotkamy sie w twoim domu. OK, kocham cie, do widzenia.

> *She hangs up.* **CHRIS** *has put his toys away.*

Thank you.

CHRIS. What did you say?

NANNY. This is my sister. I said I am coming to her house. I am Polish.

CHRIS. Is that fun?

NANNY. It's okay. Is it fun being you?

CHRIS. My mom says I could be anybody and she would love me. And then she says, it's a lot of work.

NANNY. Because of your father being dead?

CHRIS. I guess. And her work. I always have to be different places.

NANNY. He will never be a home for you.

CHRIS. I guess you could say it like that.

NANNY. But you have mother. It is important. And your uncle. *(Looking at a photo of people in a pool:)* You like swimming?

CHRIS. That's the YMCA. We play tennis there too, sometimes. I hurt my back when I was little and they said swimming would help. Mom goes with me. They just started a diving class.

NANNY. Like, from high up? I would be afraid. *(A loud splashing sound:)* Sspppshhhh!

CHRIS. *(Corrects her with a very small splashing sound:)* Chhhh.

NANNY. What is that?

CHRIS. You're not supposed to make a big splash.

NANNY. I would cry and be afraid.

CHRIS. If I ever get scared before a big test or swimming, my mom rubs my ears and says, "Just keep breathing, Chris."

NANNY. All people keep breathing.

CHRIS. I know, but my mom says, "It's fun to breathe. And it's rewarding." So maybe I breathe differently.

NANNY. She says it's part of your body, the losing of your father. She says your feeling was, like, infinity.

CHRIS. I was little.

NANNY. You're still little.

CHRIS. Yeah. I guess that's true in a lot of ways.

> *He stands up straight with his hands over his head, palms touching.*

Who am I?

NANNY. What? Chris.

CHRIS. I'm Jianguo Tong Wu. The Chinese Olympic diver. Listen.

*He makes his arms swing around and mimes
a funny little diving move.*

(The quiet sound of a perfect dive:) Chhhh.

NANNY. That was a good one.

CHRIS. I didn't keep my head right.

The home telephone rings. **NANNY** *answers it.*
CHRIS *picks up the flower and flies it around
a little more.*

NANNY. Hello. *(Very brief pause. Into the phone:)* No, the mother is driving with the uncle. *(Brief pause.)* I am the nanny. I am new. *(Very brief pause.)* He is at this address, yes. *(Very brief pause.)* Chris, they ask if you are sitting down.

CHRIS. *(A little smile, a little confused:)* I'm standing up.

Lights.

Scene Three
Hospital room. Evening.

CHRISTINE *(female, twelve to fourteen)* is lying in a hospital bed. **JUSTINE** *(female, forties)* sits nearby.

Throughout the scene, **DR. RIVINGTON** *(male, forties) is, as most doctors are, fairly occupied with note-making, checking charts, examining the patient, etc. He has a dry and unfussy way with people.*

He shines a pen light into **CHRISTINE***'s eyes. This goes on for a while.*

JUSTINE. So, I'm Justine.

DR. RIVINGTON. *(Without stopping:)* Hi.

JUSTINE. How does everything look?

CHRISTINE. I can't tell because he's shining the thing directly in my eyes.

JUSTINE. I'm asking the doctor. *(Looks at his ID badge.)* Dr. Remington.

DR. RIVINGTON. Rivington. *(Turns light off.)* It's a concussion, a pretty bad one. But, fortunately, it's just that.

JUSTINE. Oh, phew. Hey, what's the limousine out front? Looked like maybe it was some bigwig.

DR. RIVINGTON. *(To* **CHRISTINE***:)* Do you feel nauseous?

CHRISTINE. No.

JUSTINE. Is it some bigwig?

DR. RIVINGTON. It's a record producer. Do you know the name Lollipop Zefferelli?

JUSTINE. Seriously?! Oh my God. Lollipop? Is he here, really? That's so random. Is he sick?

DR. RIVINGTON. I think he's visiting someone.

JUSTINE. On this floor? He was, well – we have a little history, if you can believe it. This was after the car accident – my brother-in-law and her mom. I was so lost. Along came Lollipop.

DR. RIVINGTON. Small world. *(To* **CHRISTINE***:)* You fell at the pool?

JUSTINE. She was practicing a dive and hit her –

CHRISTINE. – Let me tell.

DR. RIVINGTON. Yes, I'd prefer if she told it.

CHRISTINE. I was practicing a dive and hit my head.

JUSTINE. That's what I was going to say.

CHRISTINE. It isn't your story.

DR. RIVINGTON. They should have helmets for that.

CHRISTINE. For diving?

JUSTINE. Little kids in bathing suits and helmets? Everyone would drown.

CHRISTINE. I'm not a little kid.

DR. RIVINGTON. *(While he's making a note:)* Since I started working here, I look at almost anything humans do and I just think, "Helmets. Everyone should be wearing helmets for this."

JUSTINE. I think the kids would all drown. It'd just be a big mess.

DR. RIVINGTON. Yeah, you said. *(More notes.)* So, anyway, you should stop with the diving.

CHRISTINE. *(Sad and pleading:)* No.

JUSTINE. Let the doctor finish.

DR. RIVINGTON. That was it, I was done – she should stop with the diving.

JUSTINE. Oh.

DR. RIVINGTON. You don't want another concussion.

CHRISTINE. That's the only time it happened.

DR. RIVINGTON. Things that only happen once can still have a huge effect on our lives.

JUSTINE. Chris, you should listen to the doctor.

CHRISTINE. You're not my mother.

JUSTINE. No, I'm not. Although who bought you a toy bunny, because you couldn't sleep? Who read you *Matt the Mouse* a thousand times?

CHRISTINE. You bought me something. Then you read me something. Thanks.

JUSTINE. *(To* **DR. RIVINGTON***:)* I was her mother's sister-in-law, through my ex-husband. Now I'm her legal guardian.

CHRISTINE. If you cared about me, you'd just say, "I take care of her." Not some whole confusing thing of ex-in-law-blah-blah-blah.

JUSTINE. You're just hungry.

DR. RIVINGTON. Are you hungry?

> **CHRISTINE** *shrugs.*

I think she's angry. And that's understandable.

CHRISTINE. You're so perceptive.

DR. RIVINGTON. Thanks. May I speak to Chris alone for a minute?

CHRISTINE. Christine.

DR. RIVINGTON. Christine.

JUSTINE. I'm the legal guardian, so I thought…but, sure, fine. I'll be outside.

> *She exits.*

CHRISTINE. *(Brief pause.)* So, what, you're going to tell me I'm lucky to be alive or something?

DR. RIVINGTON. God, no. I just wanted some quiet. *(Closes his eyes.)* I've got to close my eyes for one second, sorry. Man, it's tiring being a doctor.

> *They sit in silence.* **CHRISTINE** *is not sure how to react.*

(Rubbing his eyes, pressing the heels of his hands into them.) Did you know you were one single cell, for about forty minutes, right after you were conceived?

CHRISTINE. No.

DR. RIVINGTON. Now look at you, you know? Totally three-dimensional and rolling your eyes at everything. Maybe some unicorn patches on your backpack. Who knew that cell was going to be so interesting and brave? *(Gets back to his paperwork.)* What made you start up with diving?

CHRISTINE. I don't know.

DR. RIVINGTON. It must've come from something.

CHRISTINE. It feels like time kind of slows down. Or changes, somehow. Or it's like I'm flying. I like it.

DR. RIVINGTON. I can't imagine a kid of mine going up on a diving board.

CHRISTINE. How old are your kids?

DR. RIVINGTON. I don't have any kids.

CHRISTINE. No wonder they're having trouble with the diving.

DR. RIVINGTON. I think I have kind of timid genes. Our family crest is a curtain blowing in an open window. You're a brave person, Chris. Christine.

CHRISTINE. I'm just a kid.

DR. RIVINGTON. *(As he's making a note:)* You are trillions of cells going this way and that. Hundreds of billions of cells die and get born in you, every day. *(As he makes more notes:)* You know that thing, right?

CHRISTINE. *(Brief pause.)* I'm going to need a little more information.

DR. RIVINGTON. *(Still making notes:)* About how most of the cells in your body are completely new, every seven years or so. People wonder, "Can people change?" That's practically all we can do. *(Finishing notes:)* We want you to stay, okay? Probably just for one more day, to make sure everything's all right.

CHRISTINE. I...okay.

DR. RIVINGTON. What?

CHRISTINE. Nothing. I was glad you said "we want you to stay." It's stupid.

DR. RIVINGTON. *(Warmly:)* Awww. That is stupid. *(Makes a note.)* But, we do. I do. Oh, you want to look at this?

He hands **CHRISTINE** *a book.*

DR. RIVINGTON. It's about blood vessels. I'm supposed to read it but I don't have time. Make sure nothing goes wrong with your circulation – I don't know anything about it.

CHRISTINE. *(Little smile.)* Okay.

She starts looking through the book.

DR. RIVINGTON. *(Kind of gazing at* **CHRISTINE***:)* My wife and I want to have kids.

CHRISTINE. *(From the book:)* Wow. You could wrap a person's blood vessels around the Earth two and a half times.

DR. RIVINGTON. *(As he's making a note:)* Yeah, but you shouldn't.

CHRISTINE. Okay.

She absentmindedly rubs underneath her nose as she's reading.

DR. RIVINGTON. You know that little line underneath your nose, where you just touched? The vertical crease above the middle of your lips?

CHRISTINE. Yeah.

DR. RIVINGTON. The philtrum. Guess what it does?

CHRISTINE. What?

DR. RIVINGTON. Well, actually, nothing.

CHRISTINE. That's amazing! Can I come live with you?

DR. RIVINGTON. Each side of your face forms and grows separately, when you're in the womb. Two halfs of a face. Weird, huh? And that's where they finally meet up, the two halves, that little line.

CHRISTINE. Why are you telling me that?

DR. RIVINGTON. I don't know. You're a smart kid, insert a helpful metaphor. "It all comes together in the end." Something like that. *(Yawns.)* Whoo. Don't hit your head, anymore, okay? Play tennis or something.

CHRISTINE. Tennis is okay. I used to go to the court with my mom. My uncle David blasted classical music while we played.

DR. RIVINGTON. Cool. And wear sunscreen. And seat belts. There's only one you.

CHRISTINE. There's only one me.

DR. RIVINGTON. It's true. We could prove it right here and now with DNA, if I wasn't so tired and we had more resources and I felt like it.

CHRISTINE. Well, zero out of three ain't bad.

DR. RIVINGTON. You know, sometimes, it ain't.

He looks at her admiringly.

You know how to play chess?

CHRISTINE. No.

DR. RIVINGTON. Perfect. I'll bring my set tomorrow. Let me get your, the, um, is it Janine?

CHRISTINE. Justine. My beloved legal guardian.

DR. RIVINGTON. Yeah, her.

He sticks his head out of the room and looks.

Huh.

CHRISTINE. She's not there?

DR. RIVINGTON. Maybe she went down to the vending machines.

CHRISTINE. *(Quietly:)* This is my life.

Lights.

Scene Four
Sound studio of a local radio talk show.

> RADIO HOST *(male, sixties) is seated at a table with a microphone. He speaks quickly, clearly, smoothly.*

RADIO HOST. *(Smoking a cigarette:)* Mmm-mm. Delicious. And we have all those recipes right on our website, so take a look, and, bon appétit. Coming up on the show – talk about a role model. A tennis champion AND an honor student? Somebody pinch me – I've died from a massive heart attack and gone to heaven. Here's a commercial.

> *Lights bump down on* RADIO HOST *and bump up in a spotlight on* ADVERTISEMENT ACTOR *(female, forties) downstage, reading from a script, standing at a microphone.*

ADVERTISEMENT ACTOR. Are you tired of people thinking you're slightly shorter than you actually are? Do people come up to you and say, "Didn't you used to be married to Timothy's cousin?" Or, what about this one: you've met someone dozens of times, and, every time you see them, they still remember exactly who you are? Gimme a break. I'm Rachel Valdez-Islington and I want to talk to you today about the thing we all hold dear to our hearts, but never ever think about. We go through the mysterious parade of our days on Earth, always –

> *Lights bump from* ADVERTISEMENT ACTOR *back to* RADIO HOST, *now seated with* KRIS *(female, twenty-one), who's wearing a smart-looking tennis warm-up suit. The* RADIO PRODUCER *(female, sixties) is seated off to the side with notes and folders.*

RADIO PRODUCER. And, in Five, Four, Three –

> *She silently counts down to One and then signals "Now."*

RADIO HOST. Welcome back. I'm Paul Dupont, and this is "Listen While Your Neighbor is Talking," and I'm here today with Kris Rivington, tennis champion, model student, survivor. Welcome.

KRIS. Hi.

RADIO HOST. So, tell me – *(Working from notes:)* You were the, I'm checking this, Regional Champion, in tennis, and you're an honors student doing pre-med and – whoa! Science Expo – and, if that's not enough, you have kind of a sad story.

KRIS. What?

RADIO HOST. I don't mean sad, but, it's sad, with your parents, and then the others. How do you feel about all of that?

KRIS. All of it?

> **RADIO PRODUCER** *mimes someone playing tennis or gives* **RADIO HOST** *a note.*

RADIO HOST. When did you start playing tennis?

KRIS. I played with my mom when I was little, and my uncle was my first coach. Before that, I did swimming.

RADIO HOST. So you were always active?

KRIS. No. I could barely walk at first.

RADIO HOST. Because you were little?

KRIS. Because of my back.

RADIO HOST. What was that like?

KRIS. I don't know. Fine.

RADIO HOST. It doesn't sound fine. Not being able to walk.

KRIS. No one's born being able to walk.

RADIO HOST. Touché.

KRIS. What?

RADIO HOST. Touché has its origins in competitive fencing.

KRIS. I wasn't worried about the origin of it. I don't know if I'd be doing pre-med, or even be in school, if I hadn't gotten a tennis scholarship.

RADIO HOST. *(Looking through notes:)* When did you... Or, sorry, I have it here, somewhere.

> **RADIO PRODUCER** *holds up a card with "T or D" on it.*

Oh, that's right. Are you ready to play "Truth or Dare"?

KRIS. Sure. Truth.

RADIO HOST. Okay. Easy one. Who do you love most in the world?

KRIS. Actually, "Dare." Can I switch?

RADIO HOST. Feeling brave? Okay.

> *He takes out a small glass of dark liquid.*

This is four ounces of a very mysterious –

> **KRIS** *grabs it and drinks it.*

KRIS. Ugh, gross. Was that the dare?

RADIO HOST. Oh, listeners, would that you were watchers. All in a single gulp. Garlic, clam juice, bitters, coconut water, and buttermilk.

KRIS. If I'd known what it was, I wouldn't have done it.

RADIO HOST. Life.

KRIS. Oh well.

RADIO HOST. What a constitution. You have got some serious integrity.

KRIS. How do you know?

RADIO HOST. I'm just keeping the conversation flowing. Now, you grew up in a lot of different homes.

KRIS. Dr. Rivington was my doctor when I hit my head. He and his wife adopted me.

RADIO HOST. "First, do no harm," right?

KRIS. What?

RADIO HOST. It's the Hippocratic Oath.

KRIS. I know.

RADIO HOST. It popped into my head.

KRIS. So then you just say it?

RADIO HOST. I do.

> *Brief pause.* **KRIS** *is trying to see her life in this moment clearly and try to explain it. We hear some doubt and worry about the future:*

KRIS. The Rivingtons really encourage me. I got interested in science, maybe because they like it. I try to believe in myself because, just... I try to believe in myself.

RADIO HOST. The right little smile from someone, and suddenly we're collecting stamps, or learning to bake bread.

KRIS. I want to do drama at school, but rehearsals are always during practice. Is this fun?

RADIO HOST. Well, I get to talk to interesting people like you. And we have a veterinarian coming up.

KRIS. Yeah, I talked with him. You think I'm interesting?

RADIO HOST. Would you listen to this kid?

KRIS. *(Referring to the dare:)* I thought I was going to get sick after that stuff. So I just didn't think about it.

RADIO HOST. That's the trick. Proof positive there's nothing so resilient as a child.

KRIS. Maybe I haven't had the chance to be resilient, yet.

RADIO HOST. Who knows. I wish you all could see her. Not the person, or even the persona, but the essence. Who are you? Who is this being? Beneath the sweatsuit and broken homes, behind the personal history and hairstyle.

> **KRIS** *ties her shoe.*

Now she's tying her shoes. I love it. Metaphysics be damned, you got to keep those laces tied, right?

KRIS. *(Smiles.)* I guess you do.

RADIO HOST. So, your mother was –

KRIS. *(Interrupting:)* – They were in a car crash. Mom and my uncle.

RADIO HOST. And you lost your father when you were still a baby. Sadness drags behind you like a...

KRIS. I miss everybody but it's okay. I miss my mom.

RADIO HOST. A shoelace. It drags behind you like a shoelace.

KRIS. Yeah? Okay. I don't know what to say to that.

RADIO HOST. What do you feel like saying?

> *A "time's up" signal from* **RADIO PRODUCER**.

Thank you, Kris. I hope you'll join us again.

KRIS. Is it over?

RADIO HOST. Coming up: a veterinarian with an interesting specialty, but, before that: we all know *how* aromatic candles are made, but, have you ever wondered *why*? We'll find out after the break.

RADIO PRODUCER. And, we're out.

> *She begins removing the small microphones clipped on their shirts.*

RADIO HOST. Did you get ahold of Jack Darian?

RADIO PRODUCER. He can do four o'clock.

RADIO HOST. Can we make it five? I want to go kayaking today.

KRIS. We didn't talk about the Science Expo.

RADIO HOST. People extrapolate. They'll fill in the blanks.

KRIS. But this is my life.

RADIO HOST. *(As he's adjusting some controls:)* Well, yeah, but, we do have some blanks here, and, people don't like blanks. Luckily we have our own lives to fill stuff in with.

RADIO PRODUCER. Can we get a picture for the website?

KRIS. Okay.

> **RADIO HOST** *puts his arm around* **KRIS**, *who smiles genuinely, as* **RADIO PRODUCER** *aims the camera.*

RADIO PRODUCER. Big smile. Ah-one, ah-two –

RADIO HOST. *(Remembering something he's supposed to do, he returns to his computer:)* – Sorry, one sec.

> *Lights.*

Scene Five
A café. Late afternoon.

Music is quietly playing. **CHRISTOPHER** *[male, bookish, around twenty-seven] is reading a book of anatomy. Other books are piled on his table.* **LOUISE** *[also around twenty-seven, composed, professional, and somewhat hip] enters and sits at the next table.*

LOUISE. *(Smiles at* **CHRISTOPHER**.*)* What are you reading?

CHRISTOPHER. That's your opening?

LOUISE. Nope.

Music fades. **LOUISE** *takes out her phone and disappears into it.*

CHRISTOPHER. It's about human anatomy. It's called *Human Anatomy.*

LOUISE. *(Not looking up from phone:)* Great title.

CHRISTOPHER. I'm selling some of my books. But I wanted to look through them all one last time.

LOUISE. I was just trying to be friendly.

CHRISTOPHER. Sorry.

LOUISE. No, it's fine. I'm used to dealing with…it's fine.

CHRISTOPHER. Dealing with…?

LOUISE. Nothing. People. People who are like whatever you're like.

CHRISTOPHER. People have often noted my similarity to people who are similar to me. You really see me, don't you.

LOUISE. Hey, give me a break. I just saw a horse die.

CHRISTOPHER. What? Just, like, right on the street? That's so Dostoyevsky.

---

*A license to produce *The Underlying Chris* does not include a performance license for any third-party or copyrighted music. Licensees should create an original composition or use music in the public domain. For further information, please see Music Use Note on page 3.

LOUISE. It was on a horse farm. I'm a veterinarian.

CHRISTOPHER. Wow.

LOUISE. Well said. Can you watch my stuff?

CHRISTOPHER. Sure. Christopher. Nice to meet you.

> **LOUISE** *exits.* **CHRISTOPHER** *switches to a book about DNA.*
>
> *A* **CAFÉ EMPLOYEE** *enters.*

CAFÉ EMPLOYEE. *(Referring to Louise's bag and jacket:)* Whose is this?

CHRISTOPHER. She didn't say her name.

> **CAFÉ EMPLOYEE** *picks them up and exits.*
>
> **LOUISE** *returns with a coffee cup and a pastry.*

LOUISE. Where's…did you… *(Looks under table.)* Don't do this. Come on. Where's my stuff?

CHRISTOPHER. Sorry, someone took it. *(Points offstage.)* I think they work here.

LOUISE. You have to be kidding.

> *She exits.*
>
> **CHRISTOPHER** *goes back to reading, occasionally looking offstage.* **LOUISE** *returns with her things.*

CHRISTOPHER. Looks like you got everything back safe and sou–

LOUISE. – That's the last time I ask someone to watch my things.

> *She sits.*

CHRISTOPHER. Probably wise. You never know who you're dealing with. *(Returns to his book.)* They think the human genome is almost forty percent viruses.

LOUISE. Sorry? I didn't catch that and, also, I don't care.

CHRISTOPHER. Human DNA. It got to be what it is today, to you and me, by viruses attacking it and folding themselves into it. Forty percent of it.

LOUISE. Yeah, I know that. *(Looking at her phone.)* Why are you reading that – were you raised by humans?

CHRISTOPHER. Yeah, I was.

LOUISE. Oh, okay. Wow. New information. *(Dialing:)* Wait till you get to the placenta and the eyelashes. *(Into phone, she leaves a message:)* Where are you? I'm sitting here completely by myself.

CHRISTOPHER. Ahem.

LOUISE. *(Into phone:)* And I'm totally bored. And there's some junior scientist here, looking at me and clearing his throat. Hurry up. *(Ends call.)*

CHRISTOPHER. *(Back to his book:)* And if that's not enough –

LOUISE. – No, I think it's enough.

CHRISTOPHER. We have almost ten times as many microbes in us as cells. We're mainly viruses and microbes. Think of all that, all that non-us stuff in us, while we sit back in a chair and say, "Hi, I'm Joe."

LOUISE. I thought your name was Christopher.

CHRISTOPHER. No, it is. Chris. *(Very brief pause.)* I'm in med school. I mean, I'm doing my post-graduate stuff.

LOUISE. Been there, done that, got the refrigerator magnet and the crippling debt.

CHRISTOPHER. Well, but you went for animals.

LOUISE. Anyone who looks down on animals, or thinks people aren't animals, or vets aren't doctors, isn't going to be a very good doctor. If they even make it to their residency.

CHRISTOPHER. I'm in my residency now.

LOUISE. What luck for the sick and weary.

CHRISTOPHER. Yeah. *(Simply and vulnerably:)* I don't know if I can do it. I'm having some trouble.

LOUISE. *(Sympathetically:)* Oh, no. It's probably just because people dislike you. *(Brief pause.)* Well, it's not for everyone. It's pretty hard, with the hours.

CHRISTOPHER. I can handle hours. It's, I hate how people look at me. All the hope and trust in their eyes.

LOUISE. Hope *and* trust – yuck.

CHRISTOPHER. No, but it's just because I look busy and have a stethoscope. They know how little I can help and how afraid I am, but they keep pretending because they don't have any choice. Then I show up in the next room, looking busy and wise and weary, but only because I'm running from the last person I didn't know how to help. I don't know if it makes me feel like a fake or exactly like myself.

LOUISE. Maybe it's both. *(Brief pause.)* On my half-days off, I used to go to my parents' and wear my dad's pajamas and cry and ask for my favorite food like I was a little kid.

CHRISTOPHER. Yeah?

LOUISE. Is your family supportive? Everyone's usually pretty excited to have a doctor in the family. *(Brief pause.)* I'm Louise, by the way.

CHRISTOPHER. Hi. Chris.

LOUISE. Still "Chris"? Congratulations.

> **CHRISTOPHER** *looks at a book on* **LOUISE**'s *table. He picks it up.*

CHRISTOPHER. What's this?

LOUISE. *The Mirror in the Mirror*.

CHRISTOPHER. I can read.

LOUISE. Didn't want to assume. It's psychology.

CHRISTOPHER. I should change to psychology. I used to do sports.

LOUISE. You?

CHRISTOPHER. I look too bookish or something?

LOUISE. You look like you'd just get totally snapped in – that's mean. You might've done sports, I don't know what you look like.

CHRISTOPHER. Maybe I changed.

LOUISE. What sports?

CHRISTOPHER. Swimming, tennis. I did diving. Ten-Meter Platform diving. That's like thirty feet.

LOUISE. Am I supposed to be impressed?

CHRISTOPHER. That'd be great, yes, thank you.

LOUISE. Was it fun?

CHRISTOPHER. I was always getting injured but I learned a lot.

LOUISE. The body.

CHRISTOPHER. I know. It's like a nonstop surprise party. I thought I was going to be resilient.

LOUISE. Maybe you are.

CHRISTOPHER. My mom was a total...

LOUISE. Sorry, I should get going. *(Brief pause.)* What was your mom?

CHRISTOPHER. Just, I don't know...it's a ridiculous word. Saint? She drove me all over the place for any kind of lessons. We drove six hours to meet the Chinese Olympic diving team. When I got scared, my mom used to go like this with my ears *(Rubs his earlobes.)*. She'd do that and say, "You love flying through the air and I love you." She just wanted me to try hard and not be afraid. *(Very brief pause.)* And now here I am, afraid and not trying.

LOUISE. It sounds like you're trying as hard as you can.

CHRISTOPHER. I'm supposed to be observing a gallbladder removal.

LOUISE. Right now?

CHRISTOPHER. I got scared. I wanted someone to go like that with my ears.

LOUISE. Your mom's not around?

CHRISTOPHER. She was in a car accident. She was gone a few legal guardians ago.

LOUISE. I'm sorry. *(A small laugh.)* I'm sorry. You said it funny.

CHRISTOPHER. Yeah? I didn't mean to. I guess it's just naturally very funny.

LOUISE. No it isn't.

CHRISTOPHER. I know.

LOUISE. Sorry.

CHRISTOPHER. My uncle's sister-in-law left me at a hospital because she ran into her old boyfriend. She was a drug addict and he was a big music producer and also a drug addict, so they had that.

LOUISE. She, like, put you on the doorstep of the hospital?

CHRISTOPHER. She got me admitted and then left.

LOUISE. What was her name? Lisa?

CHRISTOPHER. Justine. Why'd you say Lisa?

LOUISE. I pictured a Lisa.

> **CAFÉ EMPLOYEE** *strikes a few chairs and tables, getting ready for closing, and the next scene.*

CHRISTOPHER. When people say, "Where did you grow up," I don't picture any actual place.

LOUISE. What do you see?

CHRISTOPHER. Little glimpses, maybe, blurry faces here and there, little times things felt calm.

LOUISE. Well, that's good. You had some.

CHRISTOPHER. Yeah.

LOUISE. *(Trying to picture her home:)* Maybe that's just how we see it and how it stays with us. Some glimpses. Some blurry calm.

CHRISTOPHER. Right when I thought I was starting to *become myself* or *get somewhere*, I'd suddenly be somewhere else with someone else asking me if I had any allergies and, "Is it Christopher or Chris?"

LOUISE. I'm sorry.

CHRISTOPHER. I'm sorry if I was rude. I'm telling you all this stuff. I'm just some person sitting in a café.

LOUISE. Me too.

CHRISTOPHER. *(Brief pause.)* So now, at the hospital, I guess I'm going to sort of erase myself, by myself. I don't even need other people to destroy my identity anymore – "I'll get it myself, thanks."

LOUISE. Just call and say you had an accident.

Her phone vibrates in her bag – a text message.

Listen, everyone makes mistakes.

CHRISTOPHER. *(Referring to her phone:)* You can check that.

LOUISE. It might be work.

> *She gets her phone out, but tries to stay with* **CHRISTOPHER***:*

Just call. I'm sure things happen all the time.

CHRISTOPHER. I just wish I had some people around me, saying, "You can do it, whatever it is." Or, "Come on, little Chris, just keep your" – *(Referring to insistent vibrating:)* You should read that.

LOUISE. Sorry.

> *She reads it and starts to gather up her things.*

A deer got her head stuck in a fence and cut her neck. It's near my brother's house. I have to get over there.

CHRISTOPHER. Okay.

LOUISE. *(Hurriedly typing a message on her phone:)* Well, it was nice, um –

CHRISTOPHER. *(Withdrawing into his book:)* – Yup.

LOUISE. Do you want to come with me? It might be a two-person thing.

CHRISTOPHER. Yeah.

LOUISE. Quick.

CHRISTOPHER. *(Packing up his stuff:)* Weren't you meeting – wasn't someone else supposed to be here?

LOUISE. I guess not.

> *Lights.*
>
> *Café music returns through the scene change and then fades.*[*]

Scene Six
A café. Evening.

Looks similar to the café in the previous scene, though dust-covered and with some changes. A single table and a couple chairs are still set up, with others having been stacked or moved to the side in the previous scene. Toward the back of the room are tools, sawhorses, and paint cans. Sound of a distant ambulance.

KRISTIN (forties) and her husband LOUIS (forties) enter with their daughter, JOAN (sixteen).

LOUIS. *(Referring to chairs and tables:)* What's the story with this? Do we have to deal with this stuff?

KRISTIN. I think the landlord is taking it.

JOAN. I smell something weird.

KRISTIN. *(Sniffing:)* It used to be a café. I bet it's got some good ghosts.

JOAN. Yeah, that's very romantic – I smell something weird.

LOUIS. A café, eh?

> *He sits down, grabs a file folder, and uses it like a menu.*

Hmm. What shall I have?

JOAN. *(Pretending to be a maître d':)* Sorry about the weird smell. Your waiter will be along shortly.

LOUIS. Excellent.

> *JOAN and LOUIS privately enjoy their little game, though it seems to have ended.*

KRISTIN. *(Joining the fun:)* Hello, sir. May I tell you about our specials?

LOUIS. Yes, please.

KRISTIN. Um. For our specials, tonight... Let's see...

> *A pause as they wait for her to come up with some specials.*

LOUIS. Just say any food.

> *Another brief pause.*

KRISTIN. There's, um... We have an assortment of fresh sandwiches.

LOUIS. *(Trying to be supportive:)* Yum. Sandwiches.

JOAN. Great improvising, Mom.

KRISTIN. I should take an acting class.

JOAN. Or a class where you learn to say the names of different foods.

KRISTIN. I actually really would like to try acting some day.

LOUIS. Another career change?

KRISTIN. No. Don't worry. *(Looking around:)* I didn't realize this place was so close to the hospital.

LOUIS. *(To **JOAN**:)* Mom did her residency at the hospital down the road. *(To **KRISTIN**:)* Right?

KRISTIN. My residency. Yuck. Was that me?

> **PAUL**, *a construction worker, enters with* **HELPER**.

PAUL. *(Referring to chairs and tables:)* I was just about to grab this stuff.

KRISTIN. Hi, Paul. Great. I want to bring some furniture in.

PAUL. The stuff outside?

KRISTIN. Yeah.

> **PAUL** *and* **HELPER** *clear the tables and chairs while the others talk.* **LOUIS** *checks a message on his phone.*

LOUIS. The labrador with the twisted intestines is okay. He's responding well to amoxicillin and an old tennis ball.

KRISTIN. I'm glad. You were worried.

LOUIS. I was. "Paco." He really looked like a Paco, too.

JOAN. Can we go now?

LOUIS. Yeah, actually, how long is this going to take?

KRISTIN. I want to see how noisy it is in here when you sit very quietly.

JOAN. Wow, fun for the whole family.

KRISTIN. When did you get like this?

JOAN. It's hormonal, I'm a teenager. Read a book.

KRISTIN. I've read a lot of books, Joan.

> *She reaches out to* **JOAN**.

JOAN. It's just a defensive gesture to get love and attention.

> *With love,* **KRISTIN** *pulls her close, into her lap.*

KRISTIN. Joanie-Joan-Joan. I wish I could just hold you forever.

> **JOAN** *pulls away, with a small smile.*

LOUIS. *(Brief pause.)* What should we pretend now?

JOAN. That this is real?

> **PAUL** *and* **HELPER** *enter, carrying a couch.*

KRISTIN. Oh, wow, thanks. We were going to get that.

PAUL. It's all right. I owe you.

KRISTIN. Thanks, Paul. *(To* **LOUIS**:*)* Do you want to go get some pizza or something?

LOUIS. Yeah, I'm hungry. Joanie, you want to eat?

KRISTIN. You're being a very good kid, Joan.

JOAN. Not in my head, I'm not.

KRISTIN. Oh, my darling teenaged daughter – who are you becoming?

> **JOAN** *thinks about the question.* **PAUL** *appears to remove some more stuff.*

PAUL. *(To* **KRISTIN**:*)* Thanks again, for the other day.

> *They all look over at him. A brief, weird pause, as* **PAUL** *has interrupted a family moment.*

KRISTIN. Yeah, of course.

PAUL. Saved my life.

KRISTIN. No. Sure.

> **PAUL** *exits.*

LOUIS. What was that?

KRISTIN. Nothing. We, he was having a little bit of a crisis. Go get some food.

> **PAUL** *enters with a stuffed chair, which he places near the couch.* **HELPER** *puts down a box, on top of which is a vase, a box of tissues, etc.*

LOUIS. *(To* **PAUL**:*)* Thanks a lot.

> **PAUL** *nods.*

HELPER. Hi.

> **PAUL** *and* **HELPER** *exit.*

LOUIS. Okay, kiddo, let's go eat.

> **JOAN** *remains sitting on a paint can or sawhorse.*

KRISTIN. You're not hungry?

JOAN. I don't eat wheat.

LOUIS. They have other stuff.

JOAN. It's just wheat in different shapes.

LOUIS. Well, I'm going to go grab some wheat shapes. Come join me if you change your mind.

> *He exits.*

JOAN. *(Moves toward couch.)* Does everyone in therapy lie on the couch?

KRISTIN. Some people just sit.

JOAN. Can I try?

KRISTIN. Sure.

> *She moves toward the chair.* **JOAN** *slips ahead of her and sits in the chair.*

Oh. Okay.

> *She lies on the couch, looking at the ceiling. She notices peeling paint.*

I need to do something about this ceiling.

JOAN. Kristin, please. This time is for you. *(Hands her the box of tissues.)* If you need them.

KRISTIN. Wow, you've really got the whole thing down.

JOAN. Why don't you want to work with Dad anymore?

KRISTIN. It's partly my back. I just can't be on my feet all day. And I want to try this. I love working with the animals at Dad's, but, I like people, too. I love people.

JOAN. Really?

KRISTIN. What?

JOAN. The other night I heard you yelling, "I hate people so much!" So it's surprising hearing you say you love pe–

KRISTIN. – You shouldn't eavesdrop.

JOAN. I had my pillow over my head.

KRISTIN. Well, still. Sometimes I think about my parents. My adoptive parents. They did as well as they could for as long as they could, without really knowing what they were doing. Like all of us, I guess. But I don't know whether to get mad or sad.

JOAN. Too bad there isn't a third feeling.

KRISTIN. *(Very brief pause.)* How'd you get so smart?

JOAN. No idea. *(Brief pause.)* You got mad at me when I broke my arm.

KRISTIN. I was worried. I never liked you going around on that skateboard.

JOAN. *(Brief pause.)* I thought you liked med school.

KRISTIN. It just wasn't who I was. One time I was supposed to help with a gallbladder operation, but the guy also had advanced liver cancer. They were doing it mainly for training and to make the family feel better. I didn't go and I got in trouble. I felt like a fake. Also, to be more honest, I don't think I was very good at it.

JOAN. You don't think the same thing'll happen with this?

KRISTIN. What? No. No, this'll be different. Bodies come and go, but the spirit, that's what I was always interested in. Or, the soul, whatever it is, people's ideas and feelings, the part of people that moves through the world and changes but also lasts.

JOAN. I'm moving and changing.

KRISTIN. I know you are, Joanie. Does it seem like I don't know that?

JOAN. *(Trying to lean back:)* You should get one of those chairs that leans back.

KRISTIN. That's when I met your dad, when I was supposed to be assisting on the gallbladder thing. He rescued a deer on our first date.

JOAN. I know. Amazing story. What did you do for that guy who was having the crisis?

KRISTIN. Paul? Who's moving all this stuff? I can't talk about it.

JOAN. Just, generally.

KRISTIN. It's confidential.

JOAN. Come on.

KRISTIN. One thing I told him, the feeling of lostness that makes him search, that voice that says, "Let's keep looking a little more," that's him, that's Paul, and he should remember that. That yes, he's the lost hiker, but he's also the search party. Eventually, they'll find each other.

JOAN. Where's that from?

KRISTIN. I might've made it up.

JOAN. It's good.

KRISTIN. Thank you, Joan. *(Very brief pause.)* Paul has a tennis court near his apartment and we played a few times.

JOAN. That sounds fun.

KRISTIN. I want to get back into shape. So I can tango!

> *She does a little tango dance move. Her daughter stares at her blankly.*

What's that look?

JOAN. This isn't a look.

KRISTIN. Okay. My elbow felt pretty good. Playing tennis.

JOAN. And on that fairly bland announcement, we're out of time. That'll be twice your weekly income, please.

KRISTIN. You're a very funny person.

> **JOAN** *cuddles up next to her mom.*

JOAN. Can you still come see my play this weekend?

KRISTIN. Yeah, of course.

JOAN. I think I'm a pretty good "Laura."

KRISTIN. You were always a wonderful Joan.

JOAN. *(Brief pause.)* What am I going to do, Mom? In life?

KRISTIN. Joanie.

> *She goes around behind her chair and puts her hands on* **JOAN**'s *shoulders.*

I think you can be anyone you want to be.

JOAN. Why would I want to, though?

KRISTIN. That's a horrible question. *(Very brief pause.)* I wish I hadn't said that.

JOAN. That would've been nice.

> **KRISTIN** *rubs* **JOAN**'s *earlobes.*

What are you doing?

> *She pulls away.*

KRISTIN. I used to love that.

JOAN. I'm not you.

> *Lights.*

Scene Seven
The stage. Tech rehearsal of a play in a small community theatre. Night.

Spotlight up on **TOPHER** *(male, mid-to-late fifties).* **RODERICK** *(male, fifties) is off to the side in the shadows. Both are dressed casually in new clothes with price tags on them.*

Scenery is being moved behind them, as this is a tech rehearsal. So the changeover from Scene Six can be incorporated into Scene Seven, which can also include preparations for Scene Eight.

The voices of **DIRECTOR**, **SOUND DESIGNER**, *and* **LIGHTING DESIGNER** *come from behind the actual audience somewhere, as if they are seated out in the back of the house.*

DIRECTOR'S VOICE. Go ahead, Topher. From anywhere.

TOPHER. Okay. *(Trying to find a good spot to begin:)* Hmm hmm hmm. He says the thing about hearing an echo, and then, okay. *(Simply:)* "Good evening, Night. What's out there? Is it just some breathing thing with the ability to hear? Or is it a being who can actually listen? I am lost. I'm lost." *(Brief pause.)* "Was there a plan, and I ruined it, or refused it? Was there never a plan? Or is there one, a perfect, grand plan that I'll never be able to see, even though I stare and stare while the moss grows over my name?"

> **RODERICK** *moves into the light. He speaks his lines loudly and in a stilted manner:*

RODERICK. "Johnny, I saw your car by the side of the road. Listen, you and I have had our troubles."

> *Out, toward* **DIRECTOR**, *with a hand over his eyes, shielding them from the light. He instantly shifts down into a conversational and quieter tone:*

RODERICK. Is that, should I keep going?

DIRECTOR'S VOICE. Hold for one second. And, you skipped, "I thought I was the only night owl around here," again.

RODERICK. *(Quietly:)* Damn it.

DIRECTOR'S VOICE. *(To someone nearby:)* We have some sound in here, right? Can we hear that?

SOUND DESIGNER'S VOICE. Yeah, hang on, one sec.

> *Sound of distant thunder. A few electronic beeps, static, then, by accident, a recording of an announcement:*

"– evening's performance of *What The Thread We Hang By Is Tied To*." Nope, sorry. "Photography and record –." Auughh, the thing won't shut off. Sorry about that.

DIRECTOR'S VOICE. Let's go with the thunder, but later. Can we hold here for a minute.

> *Maybe the lights very subtly shift here, though they remain focused on* **TOPHER** *and* **RODERICK**, *who are surrounded by half-painted cardboard sets of a park, with some bushes and trees and a bench.*

> *Throughout the scene, changes are being made by* **CREW MEMBERS**. *In part, the stage is being prepared for Scene Eight.*

TOPHER. *(Stretches his lower back:)* Whew.

> *A* **CREW PERSON** *tapes an X where* **TOPHER** *is standing.*

CREW PERSON. Sorry, I just have to…

> **TOPHER** *moves to the side.*

TOPHER. Sure.

RODERICK. You all right?

TOPHER. Bad back.

RODERICK. How long have you been acting?

TOPHER. About three minutes. I did the Christmas pageant last year. This is my second play.

RODERICK. You're kidding.

TOPHER. My daughter Joan did plays in school and I always loved going.

RODERICK. You have kids?

TOPHER. Just Joan.

> **WARDROBE PERSON** *enters and takes off* **TOPHER***'s watch, which is very shiny.*

WARDROBE PERSON. It was catching a lot of light.

TOPHER. Ah, okay. I thought I was being mugged very slowly.

WARDROBE PERSON. And I have this.

> *She drapes a sweater on* **TOPHER***'s shoulders. He puts his arms through the sleeves.*

We want to try an older sadder look.

TOPHER. I think I can do that.

> **WARDROBE PERSON** *exits upstage.*

RODERICK. *(Brief pause.)* So, how do you – I don't know what my question is – how do you make things sound so lonely?

TOPHER. I make things sound lonely?

RODERICK. When it's my line, I suddenly start shouting for no reason. You sound like a real person.

TOPHER. I was a therapist for a while, so I guess I listened to a lot of real people talk.

RODERICK. Nice. Drawing on your life. I should do that.

TOPHER. What do you do?

RODERICK. Security guard.

TOPHER. You probably have some pretty exciting –

RODERICK. – If my night goes well, and it almost always does, I don't see a single person. I don't hear a single sound.

TOPHER. Oh. I don't think I could handle that. All that time to think.

> **RODERICK** *loosens up his lips by making sort of a quiet fart sound:*

RODERICK. *"Pppbbtfff."* (*Stares out.*) Having time to think doesn't seem to bother me for some reason.

TOPHER. I just mean the ghosts.

RODERICK. You believe in ghosts?

LIGHTING DESIGNER'S VOICE. Going dark.

> *The stage goes dark.*

DIRECTOR'S VOICE. Roderick, can you go to your spot?

> **RODERICK** *moves about five feet away. A stark, weird light comes up on him.*

Just stay there.

> *The light changes, becoming more eerie. Quietly, to* **LIGHTING DESIGNER***:*

Oh, I like that.

TOPHER. (*From the shadows:*) Not ghosts. Just, people from life. And the past, kind of rearing up in your mind. I'm divorced. Separated. It was totally my fault.

> *Throughout the next few exchanges, lights will be adjusted,* **CREW** *will move past, etc.*

RODERICK. Did you fool around? Sorry.

TOPHER. No, it's fine. Yeah. With a patient. We played tennis near their apartment. Not a patient, technically, just a sad person I was talking with.

RODERICK. Oh, man.

TOPHER. Feeling like you're helping someone can make you feel attractive, you know? Like you're a good person, even though you're not.

> *He starts to walk toward* **RODERICK.**

I really hurt my –

LIGHTING DESIGNER'S VOICE. – Don't move.

> **TOPHER** *goes back to his mark and his conversation with* **RODERICK.**

TOPHER. I really hurt my wife. We worked together, too. She's a veterinarian. And my daughter. Maybe I was trying to, in some scared, awful way.

RODERICK. Why?

TOPHER. God, I don't know. I had a sort of crappy childhood. About six crappy childhoods.

RODERICK. I just had one. Actually, mine was good.

TOPHER. No, me too. There were people who were really there. I mean, we got through it, right?

RODERICK. *(A little loudly:)* "Do we actually survive, or does a version of us die and we press on with whoever's left?"

TOPHER. I liked that line.

RODERICK. I liked that whole scene. *(Quietly:)* They've cut a lot of my stuff. Probably because I shout everything.

TOPHER. So just try to go easy.

RODERICK. I do. But then I don't.

TOPHER. One thing someone told me – pretend you've been fighting and crying all night with your wife or husband, and the sun is coming up. You don't need to win anymore, you just want to be clear, to be heard, and tell the truth.

RODERICK. Yeah, got it. Good. Crying.

TOPHER. No, no, done with crying. On the verge of tears, but the other verge, the far verge. Tender, but exhausted, or, vulnerable, but economical.

DIRECTOR'S VOICE. Okay, again.

LIGHTING DESIGNER. Dark.

> *The stage goes dark.*
>
> **RODERICK** *moves to his mark. Stark light, as before, comes up.*

DIRECTOR'S VOICE. Go from "Life is everywhere" or whatever it is.

RODERICK. *(A simple and moving rendition:)* "Life is wherever we look, Johnny. I'm sorry you're hurt and lost. But for that little child of yours, she knows exactly who you are. While you're asking the night, "Who am I?" she's looking at you like you're the North Star, like you're the alphabet and the Tree of Life. She knows what your sweaters smell like, which shoes are yours, she doesn't need philosophy, she needs to see you smile. She learns life is livable by watching you live. A bird that never hears its parents sing never learns to sing. It never learns to sing out, 'Hello? I'm right up here on this branch. Isn't it a beautiful morning.' You know, the great Chinese thinker –" *(As before, to* **DIRECTOR***:)* So, question, when I'm saying all this stuff –

DIRECTOR'S VOICE. – Wow, nice, Roderick.

RODERICK. *(Looking out:)* Is my guy really into Chinese philosophy?

DIRECTOR'S VOICE. *(Flatly, a little dismissively:)* Yeah, let's think about that. Hold right there, please.

> *Some more work and adjusting of lights and the set quietly happens.*
>
> *Some light comes up. Maybe* **TOPHER** *cried, in the dark.*

TOPHER. That was good.

RODERICK. Yeah?

TOPHER. Yeah. Did it feel different?

RODERICK. No. I kind of felt totally like me, but not me.

TOPHER. It's weird, doing this.

RODERICK. Stopping and starting?

TOPHER. Just, everything.

> *Vibration in his pocket, a text message. He reads it and responds.*

RODERICK. We're not supposed to have our phones.

TOPHER. My daughter's in the hospital.

RODERICK. Oh, no. Is she okay?

TOPHER. She's going into labor.

RODERICK. Oh, wow. It's nice she took the time to tell you.

TOPHER. She didn't. We're a little estranged. This is from my wife. My ex-wife. "We're going to see Joan tonight. I'm coming to get you."

DIRECTOR'S VOICE. Dark, everyone.

> *The stage goes dark, except for a sharp shaft of light upstage.*

Is a door open? I'm getting a little sliver of... Actually, that's good. *(Quietly, to* **LIGHTING DESIGNER***:)* Can you add a little color to this?

> *A change in the color.*

LIGHTING DESIGNER'S VOICE. Something like that?

DIRECTOR'S VOICE. Yeah. That's nice. *(Very brief pause.)* It's too bad we can't somehow get the smell of nighttime piped in. Like dewy grass and cool air and some wood smoke. Like, the scary beautiful feel of the world, the way a lone kid would feel it, when life is all ahead of you and around you.

SOUND DESIGNER'S VOICE. *(Brief pause. A little beleaguered:)* Is that what, do you want me to try to figure out how to –

DIRECTOR'S VOICE. – No, no, just saying it'd be nice.

LIGHTING DESIGNER'S VOICE. Should we keep moving?

DIRECTOR'S VOICE. Yeah, let's do the end of the scene. We'll do it without the lines. And for the transition, let's just take a stab at it. Everyone leave however you'd naturally leave. Transitions are always hard.

LIGHTING DESIGNER'S VOICE. Watch your eyes.

> *Lights up.* **RODERICK** *and a group of people are onstage, standing together, looking across the stage at* **TOPHER***.*
>
> *The stage is fully set for the next scene, though Scene Eight will feature fuller, richer lighting.*

DIRECTOR'S VOICE. Great. And then everyone waves at Christopher, I mean Topher. Meaning Johnny.

> *One or two people raise their hands, not really waving.*

RODERICK. Should we actually wave?

DIRECTOR'S VOICE. No, you're fine just standing there. And we'll have music here, right?

> *Everybody onstage relaxes a bit.*

SOUND DESIGNER. I'll put in a placeholder and we'll find something.

COMPANY MANAGER. *(Offstage:)* Sorry. I've got someone here for Topher.

TOPHER. Yeah, actually, I'm sorry about this, but –

DIRECTOR'S VOICE. – We're almost done. Okay, so: tableau, sadness, waving goodbye, then everything ends and everyone leaves, transition, placeholder music, new scenery and the next thing happens.

> *The* **ACTORS** *create the final tableau again, and the lights fade. A few people wave to Johnny, as the light disappears.*
>
> *Jarringly, a bright, sharp light shines into* **TOPHER**'*s face.*
>
> *The music is wrong, clearly a placeholder, maybe surf music or a poppy dance song or kids singing a campfire song, but is somehow right in its wrongness.* * *It plays quietly.*

TOPHER. Will the actual thing be like this?

> *Brief pause.*

SOUND DESIGNER. *(Spoken quietly, as if to someone sitting nearby:)* This is only temporary.

---

*A license to produce *The Underlying Chris* does not include a performance license for any third-party or copyrighted music. Licensees should create an original composition or use music in the public domain. For further information, please see Music Use Note on page 3.

Scene Eight
A park. Late morning.

The new scenery is a real bench and a realistic-looking park setting. Maybe flat, painted trees fly out, and more real-looking, three-dimensional trees are revealed. The scene is slightly more realistic than Scene Seven, and lit for daytime and not night (as the previous scene generally was).

KRISTA *(mid-to-late sixties) and grandson* **PHILIP** *(ten to twelve years old), whose arm is in a cast, enter. We hear children's voices offstage.* **KRISTA** *is carrying a big handbag.*

KRISTA. Oh my God. Am I in heaven?

They sit, and **KRISTA** *looks through her bag.*

A good day is when you find a bench.

She looks off toward the children's voices.

Aren't they from your school?

PHILIP. I don't think so.

> **KRISTA** *finds a juice box, puts a straw in it, and gives it to* **PHILIP**.

KRISTA. *(Looking off:)* Isn't that the redheaded boy you used to play with?

PHILIP. *(Has a sip, as he looks over:)* I don't think that's him exactly. *(Referring to his cast:)* This really itches.

KRISTA. Here.

She hands **PHILIP** *a pencil to scratch with.*

Your mom broke her arm skateboarding when she was little. Hers itched so badly. I tried to get this special cream in there, but it got the cast all soggy and they had to redo it.

PHILIP. Did you ever break your arm?

KRISTA. No, knock on wood. I had to wear a thing for my back, kinda brace, when I was little.

PHILIP. Did it hurt?

KRISTA. Not really. But I was embarrassed about it. *(Brief pause.)* The time is going to fly right by. They say it grows back stronger.

PHILIP. I'll lift those kids over my head.

KRISTA. That's the spirit.

PHILIP. I'll throw everybody into the ocean. Splash!

KRISTA. What you do with your strength is your decision.

> **CHRISTOPH** *(mid-to-late seventies) enters with daughter* **JOAN 2** *(forties).*

CHRISTOPH. There's something in my shoe.

JOAN 2. We're almost there.

CHRISTOPH. Let me just get it.

> *He sits at the end of the bench.*

Hello.

KRISTA. Hello.

> *She watches* **CHRISTOPH.**

CHRISTOPH. *(Taking off his shoe and finding what was in it:)* A pen cap. That's where that went. *(To* **PHILIP***:)* Do you have anything in your shoes?

PHILIP. *(Little laugh.)* My feet are in there.

CHRISTOPH. You're a wise young child.

JOAN 2. And you're a silly old man. Hi. Come on.

CHRISTOPH. What happened to your arm?

PHILIP. I broke it.

CHRISTOPH. Ouch. Why'd you do that?

PHILIP. I didn't mean to.

CHRISTOPH. It'll grow back stronger.

KRISTA. That's what I said.

CHRISTOPH. *(Takes a good breath, relaxes for a moment.)* Isn't the bench a great invention?

KRISTA. That's also a belief of mine. *(Brief pause.)* Krista.

CHRISTOPH. I'm Christoph.

JOAN 2. Come on, Dad. Your shoes are empty.

CHRISTOPH. There's a haunting thought. My shoes are empty. This is my daughter Joan.

PHILIP. That's my mom's name.

KRISTA. My daughter, yes. Also a Joan.

JOAN 2. I can tell she must be an amazing woman. *(To* **KRISTA,** *as she takes* **CHRISTOPH***'s arm:)* Bye. So sorry. We have an appointment.

CHRISTOPH. You said we were going to get a donut.

JOAN 2. We did. We just got one. Excuse us.

KRISTA. Okay. Bye.

CHRISTOPH. *(Fussing with his shoe or a jacket zipper:)* How's it going? Okay?

KRISTA. Yes. You all right?

CHRISTOPH. I think so. Good to meet you.

KRISTA. You too.

> **CHRISTOPH** *and* **JOAN 2** *exit.* **KRISTA** *gets a tennis ball out of her bag and hands it to* **PHILIP.** *He squeezes it to exercise his broken arm.*

That's funny, her name was Joan.

PHILIP. *(Referring to the tennis ball:)* This one's really old.

KRISTA. The dog was playing with it. *(Brief pause.)* Does your mom talk about me?

PHILIP. She says you're a good pretender.

KRISTA. Ah.

PHILIP. You were a Wise Man. You had a big cane.

KRISTA. Oh, in that silly Christmas show. She saw that?

PHILIP. I did too.

KRISTA. When? I did it a few different years.

PHILIP. I don't know. When I was little.

KRISTA. Why didn't you say hi, afterward?

PHILIP. Mom said it would be hard for you to switch back and forth between different people.

KRISTA. Well, I would've loved to see you.

PHILIP. You looked happy when everyone was clapping.

KRISTA. Did I? When your grandfather and I got separated, when he moved to the little house, I didn't know what to do – and the pageant seemed fun.

PHILIP. You were in another play. For grown-ups.

KRISTA. I was.

PHILIP. Mom had a picture that was in the paper.

KRISTA. I was in the paper. That play was called *The Thread We're Hanging From*, something like that.

PHILIP. That doesn't sound very good.

KRISTA. No? It had some memorable lines. Do you know – I was working on that play the night you were born. Your grandfather came to get me. Right in the middle of everything.

PHILIP. You just left?

KRISTA. I wasn't sure your mom would want to see me at the hospital, but, yes, I wanted to welcome you into the world. So I left. Your grandfather was good like that. Remembering what's important.

PHILIP. Mom cried in every room when we were cleaning Grampy's house.

KRISTA. They were very close, Joan and her dad. They had a way of joking. Pretend we own a restaurant, pretend this is a radio show. They were always laughing.

> **PHILIP** *is moving the tennis ball back and forth in front of his eye, periodically blocking out* **KRISTA**'s *face.*

PHILIP. You're disappeared. *(He moves it toward her face again:)* There you are. *(Toward his eye again:)* Bye bye. *(Back:)* There you are.

KRISTA. Hello. *(Perhaps fighting some tears:)* I love you so much, Philip.

PHILIP. Thank you.

KRISTA. I sometimes feel surprised, being here – like I walked through a door into someone else's life. I'm sorry if I ever haven't been a good grandmother.

PHILIP. That's okay.

KRISTA. It's easy for people to forget who they are sometimes.

PHILIP. I don't forget who you are.

KRISTA. *(He happened to say the perfect thing.)* Oh, Phillie. You'll never know how good that makes me feel. Thank you.

PHILIP. I'm hungry.

KRISTA. Then let's get you something to eat. *(She looks up.)* We should've brought an umbrella. It's so cloudy, all of a sudden.

PHILIP. No, it isn't.

> *Lights.*

> *A very smooth and elegant transition, with classical music that transforms into Muzak,* *coming from a small speaker in the DMV office, as the scene begins.*

Scene Nine
The Department of Motor Vehicles (DMV).
Waiting area and service counter. Afternoon.

> KIT *(male, mid-seventies) and his daughter,* JOAN 2 *(from previous scene, but with a costume change) are sitting down, joining* DMV PATRON 2 *and* DMV PATRON 3 *(male, forties).* KIT *is wearing a comfortable old sweater. There's a sign saying "Now Serving: 115." A counter is upstage, behind which a* DMV EMPLOYEE *(female, sixties) is helping a customer,* DMV PATRON 1 *(female, teens).*

DMV PATRON 3. *(To* JOAN:*)* What number are you?

JOAN 2. One million.

> *Small laugh from* DMV PATRON 3.

KIT. What's that?

JOAN 2. He said, what number.

KIT. What's my age?

JOAN 2. No. This.

> *She points at the ticket in* KIT*'s hand.*

We're 117.

KIT. Oh, the little paper. 117.

> DMV PATRON 1 *leaves the counter and exits with a new license. Very quietly, but excitedly:*

DMV PATRON 1. Yes!

DMV PATRON 3. Remember that? Your whole life stretched out like you could fly.

KIT. I don't.

JOAN 2. Yes you do.

KIT. I do. It was wonderful.

> *Sign changes to "Now Serving: 116."* DMV PATRON 2 *approaches the counter and quietly transacts some simple business.*

JOAN 2. We're next.

KIT. *(To* **DMV PATRON 3***:)* We ran all the way here.

JOAN 2. We walked very slowly. We stopped ten times.

KIT. It felt like we were running. My foot hurt. But at my heels was the next generation, yelling – what were you yelling?

JOAN 2. I wasn't yelling.

DMV PATRON 3. And then you get here, and time stops. Or, actually, it just somehow completely disappears as an organizing principle.

KIT. We should've brought a snack.

JOAN 2. *(Reaches in her bag.)* You're going to get fat but here's an energy bar.

KIT. *(To* **DMV PATRON 3***:)* I wish they had these back in the old days.

> *He takes a bite. He looks at it.*

I could've used these.

JOAN 2. *(To* **DMV PATRON 3***:)* My dad did a lot of sports. Too bad this'll only take four and a half hours, or, he could tell you the whole story.

KIT. *(To* **DMV PATRON 3***:)* It really does, doesn't it. It disappears.

> *Sign changes to "Now Serving: 117."*

JOAN 2. This is us. Dad, come on.

DMV PATRON 3. See you later.

JOAN 2. Do you have everything?

KIT. I think so.

> *They approach the counter.*

DMV EMPLOYEE. License renewal?

JOAN 2. Yeah. My dad needs a new license.

DMV EMPLOYEE. *(Flatly:)* It's so exciting, isn't it. Old license, please.

> *She takes* **KIT***'s license and paperwork. Stamps and paper-clips it. Enters some information on her computer.*

Are you still living at 281 Johnson Street?

KIT. Just barely.

DMV EMPLOYEE. What?

JOAN 2. He's trying to be funny.

KIT. I am. Desperately.

DMV EMPLOYEE. Ah. *(Without a trace of humor:)* Live, love, and laugh, I always say.

JOAN 2. You do?

DMV EMPLOYEE. Not out loud. *(She gets a pointer.)* We need to do an eye test. Stand behind that line.

KIT. Okay. *(Puts on glasses.)*

> **DMV EMPLOYEE** *points to eye chart, fourth row of which reads "E, M, T, U, Y."*

DMV EMPLOYEE. Read that fourth row.

KIT. E. N. Is that a P? O. F.

DMV EMPLOYEE. Almost all wrong. Try the next row.

JOAN 2. Take your time, Dad.

KIT. M? I? I don't know. It's too blurry.

JOAN 2. Are those your right glasses?

KIT. I think so. *(Looks at them.)* Yeah, these are right.

JOAN 2. Maybe you need a new prescription.

> **DMV EMPLOYEE** *takes the paper clip off the license and puts the paperwork aside.*

DMV EMPLOYEE. If it's the glasses, you can re-apply.

KIT. You probably think I'm just some old person.

DMV EMPLOYEE. And what are you?

KIT. Some old person. But a different one than you think.

JOAN 2. Do you have to talk to people like that?

DMV EMPLOYEE. I really don't.

JOAN 2. Let's get out of here.

KIT. She doesn't even see me. I could be a thousand different people.

DMV EMPLOYEE. No, I see you. I see you – *(Checks the paperwork for his name.)* Christopher.

KIT. Kit.

DMV EMPLOYEE. Kit.

JOAN 2. It's all right, Dad.

DMV EMPLOYEE. Probably not the perfect time to tell you this but I have to destroy your license. *(She cuts it in half.)* Sorry. I am. Come back again.

KIT. That wasn't the point of this trip, at all.

JOAN 2. No. Oh, Dad.

KIT. How am I going to get around?

JOAN 2. You'll get new glasses. And I can drive you.

> *The sign changes to "Now Serving: 118."*
> **DMV PATRON 3** *approaches the desk with paperwork.*

DMV PATRON 3. Hey, just come back. You'll pass. You'll be exactly like the girl who just left. Skipping out the door and feeling like you just robbed a bank.

JOAN 2. That's the spirit.

> **DMV PATRON 3** *approaches the counter.*

KIT. I always thought making mistakes and messing things up would make life seem longer. Nope. I bumbled through everything so fast.

JOAN 2. No, Dad, come on. We'll get an eye appointment and everything'll be fine.

> *They begin to exit. In the background,* **DMV EMPLOYEE** *and* **DMV PATRON 3** *quietly conduct some business.*

KIT. *(Quietly:)* Damnit. Hang on.

> **KIT** *and* **JOAN 2** *sit down again and* **KIT** *messes with his shoe, maybe straightens out his sock.* **JOAN** *looks around the office.*

JOAN 2. Do you remember when you were setting up your office on Graham Street and you let me pretend to be your therapist?

KIT. No.

JOAN 2. Well, you did. I was thirteen or fourteen. I was really lost.

KIT. And I helped?

JOAN 2. Not really, no.

KIT. What a heartwarming story, Joan. Thanks, kiddo.

JOAN 2. But I knew you were lost, with me.

KIT. That was a hard time.

JOAN 2. You said something like, "Water can be a cloud, or a snowball, or a waterfall, but it's always the same stuff, it's just in a different setting, or on a different day."

KIT. Hmm.

JOAN 2. You were saying even if I changed, I'd be okay. That being me is something real and something worth being.

KIT. Well, it's true. You might've changed here and there but you were you from the day you were born. The day I looked into your eyes, and you looked right straight back, twenty-two minutes old, and I thought, "Whoa. That's a person right there. Who's this interesting person?"

JOAN 2. I wonder what I was thinking.

KIT. *(Modestly, with a little smile:)* That doesn't sound like me, the water thing. Pretty smart.

JOAN 2. Yeah, maybe I read it somewhere.

KIT. *(Trying to salvage some credit and also be gracious:)* Well, whoever said it, I'm glad it helped.

JOAN 2. Right around there, we stopped talking for a pretty long time.

> **KIT** *hangs his head.*

KIT. *(Quietly:)* I haven't done as well as I'd hoped with some things.

JOAN 2. It's been hard for me, too, Dad.

KIT. I'm sorry, Joanie. I am.

JOAN 2. Okay. *(Brief pause.)* I know when you were little –

> **DMV PATRON 3** *has finished at the desk and exits, interrupting* **JOAN 2**.

DMV EMPLOYEE 3. – See you later. Good luck.

JOAN 2. Bye. *(To* **KIT***:)* I know when you were little you didn't have anyone around, to kind of verify if you were a snowball or a cloud. To see you clearly in any long-term stable way. But I think you're doing okay. I bet it was hard but you're doing okay.

KIT. You too. Joanie.

JOAN 2. The world invented a Joan because the world needed a Joan. Do you remember saying that?

KIT. *(Wants to remember but doesn't:)* I'm glad you do.

JOAN 2. I know you tried, Dad. And I see you. I can see you.

> *Her head is kind of resting on her hand, and she moves her hand so it covers her eyes, like the peek-a-boo game.*

Where did Dad go? Where is he? *(Moves her hand away from her eyes:)* There he is. There's my daddy.

KIT. Oh, kiddo. Joanie-Joan-Joan.

JOAN 2. You haven't called me that since I was little.

KIT. I couldn't say your name enough. I wanted you to know who you were, forever.

JOAN 2. I was your daughter. And I always will be. And it's a wonderful and mysterious thing to be.

KIT. Oh, sweetie. You're going to make a blind old man with no driver's license cry.

JOAN 2. Don't cry, Dad.

KIT. I'm just starting to figure out who I am, and they take away my identification.

JOAN 2. I'd know it was you with my eyes closed.

> *She hugs her dad, out of the blue.*

That sweater has smelled exactly the same for twenty years.

KIT. Is it bad?

JOAN 2. No. It's a lot of things mixed together.

KIT. This is the best bad day I've had in a long time. "Life is wherever we look." What's that from?

JOAN 2. I don't know. You're going to change some more, Dad. But you're going to be okay.

KIT. I will?

JOAN 2. I think so, yeah.

KIT. Okay. Now, we get a donut. Right?

JOAN 2. *(As she looks for her keys in her bag:)* Didn't we just get one?

Lights.

Scene Ten
The modest living room of an assisted-living home.
Afternoon.

> **CHRISTIANA**, *eighty-two, is seated in a comfortable chair. She has very poor vision.*
>
> **LISA** *(forties) enters, putting on a sweatshirt or maybe some sort of lab coat, making last-minute preparations for a birthday party, setting out a small cake and napkins.*

LISA. Excited?

CHRISTIANA. Who's that? Lisa?

LISA. Yup, it's me.

CHRISTIANA. Is anyone here?

LISA. You are. I am.

CHRISTIANA. Is it sunny?

LISA. A little cloudy, but it's a perfect day. We'll go out on the deck later on.

CHRISTIANA. I have the party.

LISA. I mean, after.

CHRISTIANA. After.

LISA. *(Looking at some framed pictures that have been set out:)* Is this you?

CHRISTIANA. Who?

LISA. This beautiful little person holding the flowers. It looks like a swimming tournament?

CHRISTIANA. Did they bring my pictures out?

LISA. *(Looking at photos:)* Here's you with someone and you're both – is that a horse being born?

CHRISTIANA. That was with my husband. He was a veterinarian. He never liked the name "Lisa," for some reason.

LISA. Oh.

CHRISTIANA. Your name is Lisa.

LISA. Yes, it is. And yours is Christiana.

CHRISTIANA. I guess everyone has to be named something. "Lisa." It's not the worst name in the world.

LISA. Why, thank you.

CHRISTIANA. You're welcome.

> *Some voices offstage.*

LISA. I think your first guests are here.

> *A young mother,* **JENNY**, *enters with an unseen baby in a baby carriage. Is this the same mother and child from Scene One? She's wearing different clothes.*

JENNY. *(Excitedly but quietly:)* Hello. Happy Birthday.

CHRISTIANA. Who's that?

JENNY. It's Jenny and Chris.

CHRISTIANA. You didn't have to come all this way.

JENNY. Yes, we did. Where else would we come except all this way?

CHRISTIANA. Where is Christopher?

JENNY. He's right here. I was hoping he'd sleep on the trip over. Sometimes he gets drowsy in the stroller. *(Seeing pictures:)* Ooh, look at these. You look exactly the same.

CHRISTIANA. I don't know what I look like anymore.

JENNY. You look incredible. What's your secret?

CHRISTIANA. I stole from work when I was nineteen.

JENNY. What?

CHRISTIANA. My secret is, just keep breathing. My mother told me that.

JENNY. What kind of a woman was –

CHRISTIANA. – And I did. I kept breathing. I don't remember my father, but maybe he told me something encouraging too. *(Brief pause.)* I know exactly who I am, and I don't know what I look like.

JENNY. You look great.

CHRISTIANA. *(Continues with her thoughts, calmly and evenly, even a little coldly:)* I'm almost completely on the inside now. I'm going to miss my body. Going places, dancing, waving goodbye, all the different things a body can do. To think I ever had a problem with it. Too skinny, too fat, too this, "I've got the knees of a man." Oh but we had some fun. My body let me get to Rome to eat gelato. It let me climb up on a chair at my child's graduation. Be glad you have one, a body, any size shape color. Be glad you were there when the Universe was handing them out. *(Very brief pause.)* How's that, for the thoughts of an old lady on her birthday?

JENNY. Those are some serious birthday thoughts. And I just meant, yes, I can see your spirit in these pictures. I see your spirit in you.

CHRISTIANA. You mean my aura.

JENNY. What?

CHRISTIANA. Synonyms. You can call a thing a lot of things.

> **GABRIELLA** *(twenties, Eastern-European accent), a nurse, enters.*

LISA. Oh, I think you have another guest.

GABRIELLA. Hello, Christine.

CHRISTIANA. Christiana.

GABRIELLA. Sorry. Happy Birthday. It's Gabriella.

CHRISTIANA. You didn't have to come.

GABRIELLA. Yes. It was time to check, so I come.

> *She takes* **CHRISTIANA**'s *pulse.*

CHRISTIANA. *(To* **JENNY,** *in a sort of reassuring way:)* I'm being taken care of.

GABRIELLA. *(Taking out a little cup of pills:)* And now, the green ones. Here's some water.

CHRISTIANA. *(Takes the pills and drinks the water.)* There. I'm all done.

> **GABRIELLA** *is making notes.* **JENNY** *is talking very softly to the unseen baby.* **LISA** *is checking her phone. It's not really a very special moment.*

Isn't this a moment.

JENNY. Yeah?

CHRISTIANA. I wish everyone could be here. *(Brief pause.)* May I hold the baby?

JENNY. He's been fussing all day. I'm trying to get him to nap.

CHRISTIANA. Just for a little.

JENNY. You'd need to be gentle.

CHRISTIANA. I'm an eighty-one-year-old lady, Jenny.

JENNY. I thought you were eighty-two.

LISA. Eighty-two.

CHRISTIANA. Well, I'm sure it's something advanced like that. Because I can barely even do this, anymore:

> *She stands, with difficulty, and tries to move one of her arms in a sweeping arc. She is only able to move it a little bit. What she's done might be an attempt at recreating a perfect dive, but it hardly looks like anything at all, just some tiny, troubled physical movements. She sits back down.*

LISA. That was wonderful. What was that?

CHRISTIANA. *(Very quietly and simply, she's moved on:)* I don't know. Could've been a lot of things.

GABRIELLA. *(Doing more paperwork.)* You should come to my Chair Yoga class.

CHRISTIANA. That sounds very interesting but I'm not sure if I have the time.

> *A little fussing from inside the stroller.*

JENNY. *(Quietly:)* It's okay, Chris. Oh, you really want to sleep, don't you.

CHRISTIANA. Let me hold him.

JENNY. Okay. I have him all swaddled up.

> *She gently places the fully-swaddled baby in* **CHRISTIANA**'s *arms.*

There you go.

Some fussing sounds from the baby.

Hold his head.

CHRISTIANA. I know. *(She nuzzles him.)* He's so little. He smells like my mother. *(She is having some feelings.)* I know you. I know you.

JENNY. *(Worried that* **CHRISTIANA** *will upset the baby:)* Here, I'll take him.

CHRISTIANA. Just a little more. Let me be a warm place to sleep. My body can still do that. *(Talks quietly to the baby:)* A hundred people are holding you right now. A long line of creatures marched out of the sea so I could hold you right now. Our fins turned into arms so I could hold you tight. So that you may then hold whoever's in need of holding. And that's the meaning of the world.

JENNY. *(Quietly:)* Birthdays. You know, it's funny... Wait, is he asleep?

CHRISTIANA. Keep breathing, little Chris.

A tiny, contented sound from the swaddled baby.

Lights.

Scene Eleven
Waiting area. Afternoon.

> KHRIS *(male, eighties) is sitting in a row*
> *of chairs. He's blind and his white cane*
> *and a small paper bag are by his side.*
> *He can get fuzzy with the details but he*
> *speaks with clarity and without being too*
> *troubled or anxious about his mental state.*
> *A receptionist,* LANGLEY *(female, twenties to*
> *fifties), sits in a large window in the back*
> *wall.* KHRIS *and* LANGLEY, *though in separate*
> *areas, both face out toward the audience.*
> LANGLEY*'s generally busy with paperwork*
> *and office duties. Occasional muffled sounds*
> *of construction work (or Scene Twelve being*
> *set).*

LANGLEY. You found the entrance okay? *(Brief pause.)*
They're doing construction at the school next door.

KHRIS. Yup. Found it.

LANGLEY. Is this right? K, H, R, I, S?

KHRIS. Correct.

LANGLEY. I like that. What's it from?

KHRIS. My parents.

> *He checks with his hands to make sure his*
> *cane and bag are still beside him.*

I smell chlorine.

LANGLEY. They were just cleaning in here. *(Some paperwork.)*
It'll be a few more minutes.

KHRIS. Great. *(Very brief pause.)* What will?

LANGLEY. Before we're ready.

KHRIS. Great. *(Very brief pause.)* Where am I?

LANGLEY. The waiting room.

KHRIS. Of course. *(Very brief pause.)* And what am I
waiting –

LANGLEY. *(Interrupting:)* – You are, I believe – let me check – yes, you're getting a referral to see a physical therapist.

KHRIS. Right. For my back.

LANGLEY. This says for a circulatory issue.

KHRIS. As long as it's something. *(Very brief pause.)* Did you know you can stretch a person's blood vessels around the world twice?

LANGLEY. Isn't the body amazing.

KHRIS. But you shouldn't. Unless it's absolutely necessary. *(Very brief pause.)* I brought a lunch because it's always a long wait. I guess that's why you call this – bah dum dum, wait for it – an ambulatory clinic. My daughter Joan used to come with me.

LANGLEY. I think someone here can help you back to the shuttle bus.

KHRIS. My daughter used to help. With everything. With everything.

LANGLEY. Where is she today?

KHRIS. *(Partly as if he is clarifying what the question was, but also sounds a bit like he's calling out:)* Joanie? Where is Joanie? *(Very brief pause.)* She…

LANGLEY. *(Brief pause.)* Family is the best.

KHRIS. They give me parties at the home I'm in. I'm dying of cake. *(Quietly, referring to the waiting room:)* Is someone else here?

LANGLEY. Just a few more minutes. Are you comfortable?

KHRIS. I'm okay, it's just my back.

> LANGLEY *steps away from the window.*

And, according to you, my circulation. And my five senses aren't what they used to be, back when I was taking them for granted. Hello?

> *He listens for a moment. Maybe he's glad to think that he's alone. He speaks, simply, to the darkness:*

KHRIS. I flew through rooms in my father's arms. My mother held me in the pool while I splashed and kicked. This body, right here. This person, from there to here. And now to where?

LANGLEY. *(Appears in the window, picks up some files, and exits.)* I'll be right back.

KHRIS. What's that? *(Brief pause.)* I've been very lucky, Room.

> *He accidentally drops his lunch bag and a utensil to the floor. With some difficulty he gets down to feel for these things.*

(Quietly, to the lost bag:) Where did you go?

> *He moves his hands around the floor, finding something.*

Why did I bring this? A fork. For my pasta. Which is where?

> *He finds the bag and, from a kneeling position, tries to get back up, hurting his back and causing a small, sharp pain. Nothing tragic, but definitely an annoyance that makes it harder to move.*

Auughhh. *(Brief pause.)* Hello?

(To whomever might be there:) Sorry? Hello? I don't know anyone's name but can you help me?

> *Lights.*

> *As quickly as possible, lights up, or divider up, revealing an area of the stage that's already been set:*

Scene Twelve
A country cemetery. A beautiful morning.
Some birdsong.

A gravesite (a rectangular hole in the ground) and some dirt next to it, upstage. A coffin-lowering device sits over the hole (metal frame and straps). Very green grass and a lush natural environment. Over to the side is a folding table. An easel with a large, framed display of a biography and some small photos, under glass. From a distance, it's impossible to see who's in the photos. A modest flower arrangement sits near the easel.

In the background, and surrounding this event, there is much beauty, greenery, and light. Design elements should be used (subtly, thoughtfully, economically) to maximize the feeling of openness and sky, daytime, etc.

However any double-casting of the play is handled, the whole cast should join this scene. The preferred doubling is in [brackets] below.

JAKE [FATHER] *(male, thirties to forties) is looking into the grave.*

JUNE [MOTHER] *(female, thirties to forties) enters with some bottles of water, folded paper programs, snacks, and other supplies in a box. She begins arranging these things on the table.*

JAKE. It feels like a Wednesday for some reason. *[Note: On Wednesdays, he should say "a Monday."]*

JUNE. *(Checks to see if it does.)* I'm not getting that.

JAKE. *(Looks into the hole.)* Why's the box already down there?

JUNE. I let Danny go early, he's taking his wife to the airport. He lowered it down a few minutes ago.

JAKE. The family's not going to be mad?

JUNE. I don't know.

JAKE. That's an important moment for people, to really let it all out, you know? When they see the coffin get lowered into the cold ground.

JUNE. I think it'll be all right.

JAKE. Yeah, probably. Have you ever jumped down there? It really is cold ground, physically. *(Looking at the table:)* Snacks. That's good. In case there's older people. Or younger ones.

> *With spray cleaner and paper towels,* JUNE *cleans the glass on the easel display.* JAKE *looks down into the hole, again.*
>
> JUNE *is reading the biography as she cleans.*

JUNE. Stamp collecting. That's such a quiet little hobby.

JAKE. You could do it your whole life without anybody knowing.

JUNE. Is that privacy or loneliness?

JAKE. Thin line. You could have a little birthmark in the shape of a bird, or a thumb that bends in some funny way, and then, one day... *(The sadness of things hits him:)* Wow.

> *He picks a weed from the side of the grave and tosses it in.* JUNE *does some more preparation, neatening the snack table, etc.* JAKE *looks at the easel.*

JUNE. There's a person down there. A body. I don't get used to this.

JAKE. *(As he's looking at the bio:)* Where's your tennis and your japes now?

JUNE. *(Glancing at the bio as she gets back to work:)* Does it say "japes"?

JAKE. That was me. I said japes.

> *He examines the bio on the easel again, as*
> **JUNE** *fusses with flowers, etc.*

Chris was the name?

JUNE. Yeah.

JAKE. This says "Chirs." *[Pronounced: Churse.]*

JUNE. No, it doesn't. *(She checks it.)* Oh, shit.

JAKE. Oh well.

JUNE. People are going to be here any minute.

JAKE. Well, hopefully, they're Chirstians *[Pronounced: Churst-chens.]* and they'll forgive you.

JUNE. I can run over to the office. Should I change it?

JAKE. They'll know who you mean.

JUNE. Yeah, I guess.

JAKE. On the other hand, there's not much left except the name.

JUNE. I think there's a lot that's left.

JAKE. No, totally. I'm just saying they probably want it spelled right.

JUNE. I'll reprint it and tape it to the glass.

> *She exits.*

> **JAKE** *looks at his phone.* **MIKEY [CHRIS]** *(ten) enters. He goes over to look into the hole.*

JAKE. Hello. Welcome.

MIKEY. Hi.

> *He says something very quietly into the hole. We are unable to hear it. Perhaps a very muffled version of a child saying goodbye to a grandparent.*

> **POLLY [NANNY]** *(twenties) enters and quietly reads the biography.*

POLLY. This is so sad.

JAKE. *(Gently:)* We're going to fix it.

POLLY *doesn't know what he means.*

JAKE *stands by attentively.*

MARTHA [KRISTIN] *(thirties) and* **BEN [CHRISTOPHER]** *(thirties) enter,* **BEN** *with a coffee cup. People make their way to look in the hole or at the easel.* **MARTHA** *is reading the biography on the easel.*

JAKE *welcomes and directs them with gentle and respectful touches and gestures.*

MARTHA. Stamp collecting? Did you know that?

BEN. *(Reading over her shoulder:)* I definitely remember about the swimming.

MARTHA. Look.

She quietly points at the misspelling.

BEN. What? *(He sees "Chirs." Very small laugh.)* Oh.

MARTHA. *(Smiles sadly.)* Churse, we hardly knew you.

Some small laughs and smiles.

MIKEY. Don't make fun.

MARTHA. I wasn't, sweetheart – but you're right, Mikey. This is sad. It's sad.

MIKEY. It's not sad.

BEN. Yeah, it's also – it's different things.

MARTHA. And it's sad.

     EVA [KRISTA] *(sixties to seventies) enters.*

EVA. *(To* **MIKEY***:)* There you are. Michael, you are getting so tall.

She and **MIKEY** *hug.*

JUNE *enters with the corrected biography, but stays off to the side near* **JAKE**.

MARTHA. *(Looks around.)* This is a nice spot. People always say that.

BEN. Anyone would be happy here.

> BARBARA [CHRISTIANA] *(eighties)* and GORDON [KIT] *(seventies) enter. Whispers and gentle touches.*

EVA. Did you have any trouble?

BARBARA. We probably should've just walked over.

GORDON. We parked in the lot behind the shoe store.

> REGGIE [KHRIS] *(eighties) enters from a different direction.*

REGGIE. Who is that? Is that Barbara?

BARBARA. In the flesh. Reggie, it's so good to see you.

REGGIE. I'm sorry I missed the service. They said everyone was over here.

BARBARA. It was very simple. The songs were good. Thank you for coming.

> MIKEY *scoops up some dirt and throws it into the gravesite.*

MARTHA. Mikey, honey, maybe – why don't you leave that.

> *She looks to* JAKE, *unsure of the protocol.*

JAKE. It's okay.

GORDON. *(Looking at the small photo on the easel:)* I know that sweater.

> MARTHA*'s moved next to* MIKEY *and the gravesite. She scoops up a little dirt and throws it in.* EVA *has joined them.*

MARTHA. *(To* MIKEY:*)* You have very good instincts.

> EVA *picks up a handful of dirt. She notices something in it and shows it to* MIKEY. *He smiles.*

EVA. They're always keeping busy.

> *She throws the dirt in the grave.*

MARTHA. What was that?

MIKEY. A little worm.

GORDON. *(Still looking at the bio and picture:)* Quite a life. How about that for a life.

>**ALLISON [CHRISTINE]** *(sixteen) enters.*

There you are.

ALLISON. Here I am.

GORDON. You have a beautiful singing voice.

BARBARA. *(To **ALLISON**:)* You do. Those old songs. They get me every time.

GORDON. Whoever picked the music did a good job.

BARBARA. How's school?

ALLISON. Good.

JAKE. *(Gently and respectfully, almost solemnly:)* I have some vouchers, if anyone parked across the street.

GORDON. Let me grab one of those.

>*He does.*

>**BARBARA***'s sweater falls off her shoulders.* **BEN** *gently places it back on.*

JUNE. We have more food and coffee in the main building.

REGGIE. May I...?

JAKE. Excuse me?

JUNE. Please.

REGGIE. *(Begins to speak to the assembled:)* I'm sorry I wasn't able to make it to the –

POLLY. *(Having a very sad moment and hasn't noticed that **REGGIE** is speaking:)* Who sent all the flowers? The first thing I thought –

BARBARA. – Polly, I think Reggie is going to say a few – *(Noticing **POLLY***'s tears:)* Oh, sweetie.

>**POLLY** *goes into* **BARBARA***'s open arms.*

REGGIE. *(Begins again:)* Hi, hello. *(A small, sad smile.)* There's so many of these. I go to so many. Some of you younger people might not know what it feels like. And you shouldn't. You shouldn't know. *I* don't really know. *(He is fighting tears and mainly succeeding.)* I do want to tell you one thing. Two things. The first, just... it's difficult. Things are difficult, aren't they. Difficult and rewarding. It's quite an honor to be born, isn't it. And it takes some strength to live up to that honor. So, strength. And of course love. Chris... Chrissie was... You don't need me to tell you. You've got your own memories. It's hard not to feel, when I look out at everyone, the presence, or the...the presence... *(A small, difficult moment. Quietly:)* I'm sorry.

> **ALLISON** *hands him a small paper cup.*
> **REGGIE** *takes a sip.*

Oh, that's nice. Apple juice. I was expecting water.

> *Blackout.*

End of Play